Curious
Confession

Brie Kraus

To all who love a mystery.

Curious
Confession

Chapter 1

Deep in the woods of "Hartsfield" town, he leaped out of a bush and into a small puddle for a drink of water. Although it was a hot Summer's day, there were many trees which blocked the light getting to the puddle, preventing it from evaporating into the lazy air, so the area was still rather moist. The rabbit sat by the puddle for several minutes, taking occasional sips of water, watching the world go by, flies flying, creepy crawlies crawling, and leaves waving across the gentle breeze. Nothing at all could be heard; nothing but the distant sounds of life outside the woods, and the tiny movements of other forms of life nearby.

Suddenly, this peace and tranquility of a normal, natural day was disturbed by a group of youths, rushing to get out. Alerted by the sounds of the footsteps, it took action and leaped away from the apparent danger. Four people in total were there, and the rabbit watched as they shot past it, making very little noise from their mouths. Slowly, the rabbit emerged from its hiding place, and returned to the puddle. It then looked towards the distance, as it watched the four people running away as fast as they could in between the trees.

The year was 1992, and the week after that strange occurrence, a group of friends gathered in the main council estate of Hartfield. This council estate blended in with the landscape of boarded up houses with its rotted siding, peeling paint, and gray color, a stark contrast to the red it had once been, thus creating the perfect atmosphere for the drug dealers that moved in and the violence that they brought.

This did not stop a group of seventeen year olds from leaving their homes during the day, or the night. Five boys and two girls stood outside one of the boys' homes, standing around, doing very little, like teenagers do. Four of the boys, Josh, Steven, Daniel and Richard, were the best of friends; they had always been together since childhood, and were never seen without one whenever they left the house. Moira and Libby, the two girls, were good friends, but not best friends. In fact, the only thing that connected them was the other boy, John. He lived in the street, and stood outside his house, wondering what on Earth he was doing, talking to the other boys. Moira was John's cousin, and Libby was a friend, or a potential love interest, as some would see it.

"So, are you going out with your girlfriend today, John?" asked Steven, mocking John and Libby for been such good friends.

"Shut up, Steven!" Libby cried, determined to not let him get to her.

"Don't start on me!" screamed Steven, who did not want to be shown up in front of his friends.

"Alright, alright," Moira said, trying to calm everybody down before, yet, another fight started.

"My mother will not like you saying those things," said John, who was scarcely able to control what he said.

There was silence, and both Moira and Libby stared at John. The four other boys just burst out into a fit of laughter.

"That's not funny," said Libby, "you're all sick for laughing at such a thing!"

"He's such a weirdo!" cried Richard.

"No he's not," said Libby, moving closer towards John.

"Are you two together forever?" laughed Daniel.

Libby was so outraged by now. She did not want to let anybody hurt John, because she was in love with him. Moira saw this, but she cared about other things too much, so she let it slip from her mind.

"Why are you standing there doing nothing, John?" Moira cried, trying to get her cousin to fight back.

John just stood there, motionless. He did not know what to do in this situation. He had never once considered or planned what to do should this situation arise in his life, so he had to be spontaneous, and he stood and thought, doing nothing else.

"For once in your life, just stand up to them! And Richard, you should be ashamed of yourself!" Moira added, looking at Richard, "I thought we were friends!"

Richard continued to laugh. "I'm sure you'll get over it by tomorrow!" he said, winking at her.

Bored of messing around with a social outcast, the boys decided to leave When they left, Moira knew that she had to do something to calm John down, so she started a new conversation.

"Anyway," said Moira, "are you thinking of coming to my friend's mother's wedding anniversary in a few days' time?"

"I don't know," replied Libby, "I don't really know them that well."

"I suppose, but there is also Mr. Block's 100th birthday on the same night, so it is going to be very busy! Almost everybody in Warwick Road will turn up!"

"I'm not sure. I might be working yet!"

"You're working now?"

"Yes!" cried a proud Libby, "I think so, anyway. I've been looking for some work experience recently, and the agent who is helping me has found a few jobs for me to do. Mainly in hotels. It's somewhere to help get me started."

"That's brilliant!" cried Moira, trying to remain talking to distract John until he had forgotten completely about the event that had just occurred.

John remained silent throughout the conversation, even though he stood in between the two women.

"Anyway," said Libby, "I'd best be off!"

When Libby left, Moira talked to John.

"Have you taken your tablets?" she asked him.

"Yes. You know I always take my tablets," replied John, "what sort of mother do you think my mother is if she does not allow me to take my tablets?"

"John, we've been through this..."

"And I'm telling you, my mother is not dead!"

"She is!"

"She's in the house, right now!"

Moira shook her head. She was beginning to get increasingly worried about her cousin. "There's no talking to you, is there?" she said to him, almost crying.

John did not seem to hear. Instead, he cried, "I'm coming mother!" leaving Moira on her own.

Moira then turned to the house, and looked in the window of the bedroom where her dead aunt used to sleep. She could not believe her eyes for a second, when she thought she saw the curtain move. It was only for a fraction of a second, but she knew it could not have been John because he had only been in the house for two seconds. Moira thought nothing of it and went home, worrying about John's welfare.

Several days later, the body of Josh Dowling was discovered in the woods. Then, two days after that, Steven Burbery. Daniel Gibson's body was found two days later, and five days after that, Richard Cliffe. All four had been knifed to death, and all had been discovered in the woods, just outside of town. The police had no leads at all—there was no DNA evidence, and a that handful of statements were not enough to solve the murder, so the files were packed in a box and put with the rest of the unsolved murders.

Of course, people had their theories, but no evidence to support it. Everybody else in the world forgot about the murders; everyone, except those in Hartfield. No one ever dared to speak of the murders, because many people on the estate knew the families of the victims rather well, so it had affected them personally. Although everybody wanted to know who the murderer was, not one detail emerged about the character of the killer. Nobody knew anything about this person other than their local brand name—the 'Hartfield Hacker'.

Chapter 2

It was a dreary November afternoon in 2012, and the team and I had finished for the day. It was another boring day, as usual, because it was just the usual: going out to investigate a murder, waiting for a opst mortem, looking around the crime scene for evidence, and securing it. Nothing else was involved in my job. Sometimes, I would interview the killers, but that was usually done by another person. I was sick of my job already, and I was only three months in!

I sat at my desk, like the others, having a conversation, before packing up my things to leave for the night. However, we were not allowed to leave the building for another five minutes, so I and my four colleagues decided to chat to pass the time.

The first was Miranda, a woman in her thirties, and she looked the most professional out of all of us. She had long, black hair (which she sometimes tied) and she wore very little make-up, although she did not need to wear much. She wore the same business-like clothes every day, and she was determined to solve any murder that came across her. She was a bit like me, in a way, but Miranda had more experience than me, even though I could not tell which of us was the best detective. She often talked about her achievements, although she did not brag about them. One of the pictures on her desk was one of her winning an award, but I never knew what. She was friendly, but best to not make an enemy of her.

The other woman in the team, aside from me, was Patricia Hobsworth. She was the deputy head of the team, and had the typical appearance of someone in their late fifties, plump, with short, blonde hair. If you listened to her speak, you would never guess that she had done so well in life, because she sounded like a stereotypical, northern housewife.

Then there was Graham Mitchell. He originally came from America, and had lived in Britain for about thirty years. He was in his late forties, even pushing for fifty, and was very tall, with long, brown hair. He was a fun-loving person, and tried to lighten the mood slightly. However, he seemed to stand in the background, when I was partnered up with him for some murder investigations. Perhaps he was not confident enough, or perhaps he was not cut out to be a detective. I had nothing against him, but I just thought that everybody else in the team was more intelligent.

Finally, there was the boss, Clive Mitchell. I sometimes got confused because there were two people with the same last name on the team, but since we had to address the boss as DI Mitchell, we just decided to call Graham Graham, and he was more than happy with that. I struggled to form a reasonable opinion of the boss; he seemed to have no personality at all. I spoke to him only when I needed to. I had never had a proper conversation with him. He was always very dull and depressing to be around. Perhaps that was just his way, and he might have liked it like that. I think that everybody else on the team felt the same, because they hardly spoke to him either. I had heard that he had a family, and surmised that that was the reason for his standoffish behavior. I never found out, though.

Just before we left, I decided to ask the others about their past experiences before entering this job, because although I had worked with them almost every single day for three months, I hardly got the chance to chat to them.

"So," I asked everybody in the team, excluding Clive Mitchell, who just sat in his office reading a magazine with a big busted woman in a skimpy bikini on the front cover, "what did you all do before this job."

"Well, Tammy," begun Miranda, "I was always a police officer, from my early twenties. I worked my way up from there. I was always so passionate about solving crime."

"I see what you mean, but I wasn't always passionate about crime solving," I replied.

"No?" asked Miranda, showing an intrigued look on her face.

"No. It was only a few years ago when I solved my first murder."

"But you weren't a detective then?" Patricia said, joining in with the conversation.

"No. I was seventeen at the time," I replied, trying not to look too proud of myself.

"I think I heard about that," said Patricia, "and I have also seen you in the newspaper a couple of times. You were the one who solved the Alesha Christen case, weren't you?"

"I was," I said, feeling rather modest about my accomplishments.

"Well, there's nothing that complicated in this job," said Graham, who had also read about the Alesha Christen case. "It's just the same old thing in here."

"What about you, Graham?" I asked, "what did you do before you came here?"

"I was a police officer for a lot of years," said Graham, "and I just worked my way up from there."

"Can I ask you something?" said Miranda.

"Fire away," I replied, knowing what Miranda was about to say.

"I don't mean to be rude, or anything, but how did you get the job without becoming a police officer first?"

"I knew you were going to ask that," I laughed. "Well, I was fairly lucky, actually. I got my degree in criminology, and I joined the police force for a couple of months, and then the boss just went up to me one day and said, 'do you want to be promoted to a detective?' I was so shocked. I thought that it took years of being a police officer to become a detective."

"It usually does," said Miranda, trying not to sound resentful or jealous of me for becoming a detective so quickly.

"They must have saw your potential," said Graham, "I mean, they must have known how good you were at solving murders."

"Yes," said Patricia, trying to move the conversation on. "Anyway, like Graham said, this job is so boring. Nothing exciting happens here."

"I love a challenge!" I cried, desperate for something unique to come along. "I'm sick of these gang killings, day in, day out. Can't they just all make peace?"

"Then we'd have no job!" laughed Patricia, switching the television on. "Here's something for you to watch."

It was the six o'clock news. I had not noticed this morning before I went to work what day it was. On the television, the news anchor said, "today is the twentieth anniversary of the first killing in Hartfield. Twenty years ago, today, Josh Dowling was brutally murdered in the woods on the outskirts of Hartfield, a small town in Manchester."

"That's near us, isn't it?" asked Graham.

"Just a couple of miles away," replied Patricia.

The newsreader continued to speak. "To this day, the killer, known as the 'Hartfield Hacker', has never been caught, and the families of the victims are still fighting for justice, but with no DNA evidence to link anyone to the murders, it is unlikely that the killer will ever be found."

"It's so awful," I said, feeling sorry for the relatives of the victims.

"It boils my blood!" cried Miranda, "just knowing that the killer is still out there makes me feel sick!"

"The killer might be dead now," said Patricia, trying to reassure Miranda.

"It's a shame there's nothing we can do for them. We have no leads whatsoever. Their files are just packed away in a box somewhere, like many others," added Miranda.

"Anyway, it's time to go," Graham said, before he got too down.

I was the last person to leave the building, since everybody else was so eager to get home. Even the boss left before me. I suppose that was a good thing, since it showed that he trusted me. I took my time, since I had nothing to look forward to. I was going to call my mum, and that was it. Even though we lived in the same city, we were a fair distance apart, so I did not really get to see her that often, because I had lots of work to do. Still, I was proud of my job and it made me happy, so it was worth it.

After I packed my things, and put on my coat, I was ready to leave, but as I put my coat on, I saw somebody enter the room, a person who I had never seen before in my life. He was of average height, and he had gray hair. It was very difficult to tell how old he was, because when I first looked at him, he seemed rather young, but after a couple of seconds, he looked very drained and ill. His face was as white as a sheet. He was dressed all in black: black trousers, a black coat, and even a black bowler hat, which he took off when he entered the room. This mysterious figure seemed to be apprehensive about something, but I didn't know what.

"Can I help you?" I asked him, trying to get more information about his character.

He tried to speak, but he could not, for when he opened his mouth, his voice quivered.

"Y...y...y..no...i don't know!" he cried.

"Take your time," I said. I was beginning to get nervous myself, and I didn't know why. There was something odd about this man, and I wanted to know what.

"Well..."

"Have you come here to report a crime?" I asked him, seeing that the man was in shock for something.

"No," the man replied quickly, "well, yes."

I was very intrigued and confused at this point. I really wanted to know what he wanted by now.

"Have you just seen something?" I asked him, "or has somebody just done something to you?"

"Give me a minute," the man said, "I'm not sure I want to do this."

It was only now I realized he was shaking vigorously. He was clearly a man who was mentally ill. He then put his head in his hand and scratched his forehead with his fingertips, showing that he was thinking about something, or that he was very stressed.

"Don't worry," I said, "you can talk to me."

"Well, I don't know how to put this, but..."

"Yes?" I said, growing more and more desperate for an answer.

"I am the Hartfield Hacker!"

Chapter 3

Clearly, this was a massive shock to me. Two minutes earlier, I had heard about the killings, and the person stood right in front of me claims he was the one who caused it? I was just lost for words. The man in question just stood there, with his hands out, implying that he wanted me to arrest him. I had no choice but to do so, so I signaled to the officers on night duty to come in and keep an eye on him through the night. I also suspected that he might commit suicide while in custody, so I made sure that he was on suicide watch before I returned home.

On the way home, I almost crashed my car due to not concentrating on my driving; I was more focused on what had just happened. This was the first truly dramatic event that had occurred whilst I was in the police force. I was beginning to become excited with the thoughts of the future. Could he really be the killer, and after all this time, could the parents of the murdered boys get justice? I was hoping that I had what it took to solve the murder. Of course, it could have been a hoax, and the man could have taken drugs, or was completely deranged, so he may have not murdered anyone at all. I just had to wait until morning, because it was a lead, either way, and that was the most important thing for now. I knew I had to sleep on it, and I had to think of things to say to him, if I were the one to be interviewing him.

Morning arrived, and when I went into work, I told my colleagues the news. At first, none of them believed me, but after a few seconds of thought, they realized that I was deadly serious about this. I would never joke about something like that, and they knew it.

"What on Earth?" said Graham, breaking the silence, "why would he do that?"

"Well, it was the twentieth anniversary yesterday," said Miranda, "perhaps he just wanted to play a huge prank on us."

"Yes, but why?" I said, fairly confused about the whole thing. If he was not the killer, why would he get himself into trouble for wasting the police's time? Still, there was a case a few weeks before that when somebody claimed they saw a murder, and there was no such thing, so there are people out there who were capable of making up stupid things like that.

"I think it's too early to judge yet," said Patricia. "I want to hear what he says first."

"And there might be a way of catching him," I said.

"What is that?" asked Patricia, who had not thought of the obvious.

"Well, I don't think the press released how the boys were killed. If the press did not give these details, then we can find out whether this man is lying or not. If he truly wants to make us believe that he is a murderer, for whatever reason, we can catch him out."

"That's a good idea," replied Patricia, "but it will not necessarily work. We have to wait and see how things turn out first."

The boss arrived, and would be the one who chose who to interview.

"Right, I've heard the news," he said, "and obviously, this is a very big deal. Soon, the press will arrive, and they will want to know all of the details."

"How will they find out?" I asked him, not intentionally interrupting to be rude.

"These things get around, Williams, and quicker than anyone would expect. As I was saying, this is the biggest case we've had in years. I don't want to put pressure on you all, but it is imperative that this gets sorted out. The families of the victims will be waiting to find out more, so even if this does turn out to be a hoax, I want it done quickly!"

The four of us just stood in silence, listening for what he had to say next.

"And I've decided who will interview him. Williams, since you've already been acquainted with him, I have a feeling that he is most likely to talk to you. Make sure you ask the right questions, and don't screw things up!" Mitchell said.

"I won't, sir," I replied, eager to talk to the apparent serial killer, though apprehensive at the same time, because this could have been it; the people of Hartfield must have been waiting for twenty years to find out the truth about the disruption of their small town, and this may finally provide the wanted answers. To be frank, I would have been bitterly disappointed if it turned out to be a hoax, and would have done everything in my power to make the sentence as long as possible for the person who wasted valuable police time. I didn't even know his name, so that was where I needed to start.

He was ready. Whoever this man was, he was sat in the interview room, waiting for me to come in and interrogate him. Before I entered the room, I looked at him through the glass window, watching his every move, trying to read his twitching face. Nerves dictated his demeanor as he tapped his left foot, and his fingers moved around his hands in rapid secession.

"Funny, isn't it?" said Miranda, "we complain that we don't get a challenge, and the next day, this happens!"

"Yes," I said, more concerned about what I was going to say to him. I had interrogated several people on numerous occasions beforehand, but this was different, though I didn't know why. Tired of waiting, I decided to get it over with and talk to the potential, infamous Hartfield Hacker.

I entered the room, and he looked at me, his eyes those of a predator. I said nothing, and neither did he, until I sat down in the only other chair in the room on the opposite side of the table from him. No tape recorder was present for the time being, because it was only the start of the investigation, but there was CCTV watching us.

"So, are you going to tell me your name?" I asked him, unsure about his reply.

"John Doe," he replied quickly.

"Well, that's really original, isn't it?"

He said nothing. He did not look at me. Instead, he stared at the floor.

"What's your real name?" I asked him.

"John Doe," he replied, annoyed.

"So, John," I said, with sarcasm, "what made you come into the police station last night and confess to the murders?"

"I...I don't know," he replied, "I...oh! The guilt was too much for me! I couldn't take it anymore."

I froze for a second. His actions were unusual; seriel killers do not feel remorse for their victims.

"OK, so you decided to come on the twentieth anniversary of the first killing?"

"Yes."

"Any particular reason for that?"

"No."

"Do you want attention or something?"

"No!"

"So, you're telling me, that it is just a coincidence that you just happened to confess to us on an important anniversary?" the frustration in my voice evident. Something told me that this was going to be a long interview.

He nodded, but his fidgeting conveyed uncertainty.

"So, you are genuinely the murderer?"

"I am," he said, looking me right in the eye for the first time.

That shocked me. I did not know why, but I felt goosebumps when he said that. It was like some other presence in the room urged me to believe him.

"So, this is not just a hoax?" I asked him.

"No! Why would I do something like that?" he asked me, looking dead serious.

"Well, other people have done this sort of thing in the past, mainly for media attention. Do you get noticed, John?" I said, the pitch in my voice wising.

"I am not making this up!" he yelled, getting more and more furious.

"Alright, calm down. You just have to understand our point of view. You see, we are not sure that you are the killer yet, because we have no evidence either way, other than your confession. So, do you want to move on to that now?"

He nodded, again looking at the floor. His body language showed me that he seemed remorseful, or ashamed at what he had done, if he had done anything at all.

"Right," I said, trying to think of a way to phrase what I was about to say, "I want to know about the details of their death. How did you kill them?"

"I stabbed them all to death," he said, as plainly as he could.

Again, I felt that sort of presence on me. Inside, the nerves in my arms were shaking. The feeling was awful. It was just the way he said that. It was like someone would say, "I got a drink," just in a casual tone as though he saw no wrong in what he did.

"Could you go into more detail?" I asked him, pulling myself together.

"What do you mean?"

"Well, I want to know where it happened, how you covered it up, and anything else you want to tell me. Let's start with the first murder. Go into as much detail as you can, if you want to prove you are the killer."

I felt like I was getting somewhere now. I wanted to see if he knew the specifics of the deaths, because details like these are rarely, if ever, released to the press. At the same time, Graham looked for police records, and Patricia was searched for the press records, to see if these details were actually released into the press, so I knew that it was important to get as much information as possible from this man.

"Well, in the first murder—that was Josh Dowling, I think. Yes, it was. It was at a party," he started.

"OK," I said, writing things down in my notebook.

"I think it was someone's birthday, or something. Anyway, I wasn't invited, but I was there, watching him from the darkness. He was just chatting to people, and did dances, and things, like any normal party. I remember he did this really funny chicken dance. Oh, sorry, I'm going off track here."

"It's OK," I said, trying to make him as relaxed as possible.

"Anyway, he went outside for something, probably a cigarette, and I called his name. Nobody else was around at the time. I then grabbed hold of him and stabbed him several times. Since this club was just outside of the woods, I had little trouble putting him there."

"Why the woods?" I asked him, feeling like there was some significance.

"I...I don't know. I just did," he said, looking very unconvincing.

"Is there anything else you'd like to add?" I asked him.

"Not for that one, no," he said, "that was a pretty simple murder."

"OK, so are you going to talk to me about the second one?" I asked him, feeling awkward about the nice, peaceful tone of voice I had to use when discussing something as horrific and violent as this.

"Well, in the second murder, that one was really simple as well. I watched him go out with his dog for a walk, and I followed him until he reached the woods. This took a while, but I'd been watching him several times, and he liked to go out on big walks, anywhere and everywhere. Anyway, I followed him until there was nobody else about. I then jumped on him and stabbed him to death. I left the body there, and there was no other sign of life around, but the dog."

I just sat back. This was extraordinary. I could not believe what I was hearing. This was the first time, in all of the murder cases that I had come across, that the killer actually confessed without any evidence against them.

"Can I move on to the third murder?" he asked.

"Of course," I replied, letting him do all the talking.

"Well, the third one was quite risky. I was following him, hoping for him to go into the woods. I knew he would probably go into the woods a little bit because it was a shortcut home from school. School used to end at four o'clock, so it must have been about five past four. Anyway, he walked through an open street, but he saw me with the knife! He asked me what I was doing, and I couldn't think of an excuse on the spot, so I knew I had to kill him there and then!"

I was shocked at how well he spoke. It was like it was scripted and rehearsed, everything he said. Perhaps he had prepared what he was going to say before he come here.

"Is there anything else you'd like to add on that one?" I asked him.

"No, except I had to leave him in the street because I knew that somebody in the houses opposite had probably been watching."

"That's strange," I said out loud, unintentionally.

"What is?" he asked.

"Are you sure nobody saw you?" I asked him, quite puzzled by what he had said.

"I don't think so," he said, "but I don't know."

"Was this a quiet street?"

"Yes. It was really quiet, actually. I couldn't see anyone in their houses."

"And the fourth murder?"

"This was the final one," he said, rather enthusiastically, "and in this one, I had to set a trap for him."

"Go on," I said, interested to find out what he had to say.

"Well," he replied, "I had seen Richard flirting with another girl, so I wrote a fake love note asking for him to meet up in the woods."

"How did you get it to him?" I asked, feeling like I was on top of the case.

"I slipped it through the vent in his locker, when nobody else was there. There was no CCTV at the time, either, so I was very lucky."

"OK," I said, "and then what happened?"

"You know the rest. After school finished, I watched him walk into the woods, where he expected to meet his crush. I then stabbed him about eight times, like the rest of them."

"You stabbed each of them eight times?"

"Roughly," he replied. He looked like he was been honest about the whole thing. As time went on, and he spoke more and more, it became less and less likely that he was making the whole thing up. I half-expected him at any moment to jump up and say, "Haha! This whole thing was just a joke!" But, he didn't.

"So, there is nothing you want to add about any of the murders?" I asked him, ready to take more notes.

"If I think of anything else, I will tell you."

"OK. Let's move on to motive," I said, ready to finish the interview, "why did you choose to do this to those people?"

"Well, Josh, Daniel, Steven and Richard were always making fun of us."

"Us?" I asked, intrigued by the possibility that this man had friends.

"Me and my friend, Libby. I don't see much of her now."

"Alright. What things did they do?"

"They used to play little pranks on us, but it was me in particular. About a week before the first murder, the group of them grabbed hold of me and threw me in the river in the woods!"

It was then when I clicked. I had established a connection between the places where three of the four bodies were found, and the motive for murder.

"They sound very immature," I said, trying to keep him talking.

"Yes, and I had this all of the time."

"Well, that's about everything I have to say to you at this moment in time, but I will definitely come back to you later. What's going to happen now, is you are going to get charged, and we'll look at this in more detail. Do you understand?"

He nodded.

"There is one more thing I would like to ask you," I said.

"Fire away," he said, clearly trying to make light of the whole situation.

"Do you take medication for anything?"

"Yes," he replied, "because I am a schizophrenic."

"Alright," I said, knowing that my suspicions had been confirmed, "so does anybody look after you?"

"My cousin. Her name is Moira."

"Does she know you are here?"

"No."

This was very interesting. I now wanted to talk to Moira to see what she had to say about the whole thing. I left the room, and talked to my colleagues. Graham and Patricia had returned with the news we had all been waiting for.

"He's not making it up!" cried Graham.

"Right," I said, getting very excited.

The five of us gathered round in a circle, looking at all of the evidence collected at the crime scenes. In the witness statement of the first murder, it said that Josh Dowling did a chicken dance before he left the building. That was exactly what 'John' said. In fact, everything that 'John' said matched the details of the murders. The number of stab wounds matched, as well as the locations where the bodies were found, and times of death.

"Furthermore," said Patricia, "none of these details were released to the press. I triple checked."

Curious Confession

"You know what this means?" said Miranda. "The man in that room is the Harfield Hacker!"

Chapter 4

We wanted to charge this man, but realized that we did not know his real name! We needed to contact someone close to him, and in the interview, he said that a woman named "Moira" cared for him, who was his cousin. However, there was no way that we could trace this Moira since "John Doe" failed to provide more information; he did not even have a phone number, nor did he tell her that he was coming. So, we asked him where he lived, and, to our astonishment, he told us. He said that Moira did not live with him, only that she checked on him three times a day to make sure he was alright. Mitchell sent Graham and Miranda down to the house, while we waited for new information. As a matter of fact, I wanted to speak to Moira myself. Did she know that he was the killer all these years? I just thought that it was very unlikely that twenty years had gone by and not a word had been said to connect him to the murders. Although, it was probable that Moira knew about this.

Within thirty minutes, Graham and Miranda arrived back at the station with Moira. I was ready to ask her a few questions about this, and hopefully, the answers would shed more light about "John's" life. When Moira entered the room, her middle-aged face, which contrasted sharply with her lean, tall frame and wiry, long black hair, put me at ease with its friendly smile, but I knew that such things could be misleading.

"Hello, Moira, I'm Tammy Williams," I said, trying to take things slowly.

"Can somebody tell me what this is all about?" Moira said, looking very agitated and confused.

"In a moment," I said, knowing that what I was about to say to her may have shocked her.

"Why am I here?" she continued, "and where is John?"

"John?" I asked, not knowing that his real first name was actually John.

"My cousin! He's has problems, and he's gone missing!"

"Did you report this to the police?" I asked, going into a little bit more detail with things.

"No," Moira replied, "I thought he might turn up again. This isn't the first time he's been here."

"Is John a schizophrenic?" I asked, diving right into the investigation.

"How did you know?" said Moira.

I wanted to keep her as calm as possible.

"Well, I've got some bad news for you," I said, "so prepare yourself."

"He's dead!" she screamed, letting herself get out of control.

"No!" I said, rather firmly.

"He's done something, hasn't he?" said Moira, with a tear in her eye.

"You could put it like that," I said, trying my best to prepare her for what was about to come.

"Will you just tell me?" said Moira, impatient and anxious to hear the news.

"Well, John came to us last night, and, do you know about the Hartfield Hacker?"

Moira looked at me, still puzzled.

"Yes?" she said, her voice tight and more of a whisper.

"Well, he's confessed to those four murders."

Moira said nothing. She just sat there, her face motionless. Her eyes were still, staring down at the floor, and her mouth never moved. It was like looking at a photograph. Not one part of her body moved, and for a second, I thought she had died of shock. I decided to leave her for five minutes, and I made her a cup of tea.

When I returned, she appeared to have processed the news some, even though she still looked very bewildered.

" Moira," I said to her, ready to move on, "you are not under arrest, and you are free to leave at any time."

"Is John here?" Moira asked, the second I finished talking.

"Yes, but you can't see him yet. Do you understand?"

Moira looked disappointed, but she nodded, not bothering to look in my direction.

"I'd like to ask you a few questions to help us with our inquiries."

"What proof have you got that it's him?"

"Well, we have quite a bit of evidence, actually," I replied, "and I will come to that in a moment. For now, I want you to answer these questions as truthfully as you can. Can you do that?"

Moira nodded.

"Alright then. Let's start with John's name."

"What about it?" asked Moira.

"Well, what's his last name?"

"Doe," replied Moira, not twitching one bit. I was not expecting that reply. So, John was telling the truth about his name.

Moira continued to speak. "I know it's a stupid name, but that's his name!" she added, almost crying.

"OK, and are you his care giver now?"

"Yes. When my mother died, I stepped in. There's nobody else now, you see."

"Alright, Moira, and how long have you been caring for John?" I asked, still bemused about his name.

"About two years now."

"And you come in to see him three times a day?"

"Yes. Has John told you that?" said Moira, eager to know what John had been saying.

"He has," I replied, unwilling to give away any more information, "and how long to you visit him every time you come in?"

"It's only a few minutes at a time," said Moira, "he can pretty much look after himself. I make sure he takes his medication. He's fine when he's on the medication."

"Have there been any times when he has not taken his medicine?"

"No," Moira replied.

"I'm going to ask you some personal questions, now, alright? And I don't want you to be offended. I just have to ask you them, OK?"

"Alright," said Moira, appearing to be nervous.

"Well, has John ever talked to you about the murders at all?"

"No," said Moira, quite unconvincingly.

"Have you ever seen these murders mentioned on the television, or radio when John was around?"

"No," said Moira, "you don't understand. Nobody in Hartfield says anything about these murders! It's like, if we say it, it's a curse on the town! I can't explain it!"

"I sort of see where you are coming from," I said, agreeing with her. It was true that when a murder occurs, nobody in the area dares to say anything about it, in case it would cause a stir or upset anyone.

"You don't think I'm involved, do you?" said Moira, beginning to get rather excited or worried.

"Not at the moment, because there's no evidence against you," I said. "I'm just trying to establish what life was like for John, and his character."

Moira said nothing. She sat back in her seat.

"Moving on now," I said, not wanting to go down that avenue, "what was your relationship like with the victims?"

"Well, it was a long time ago," said Moira, showing that she was thinking, "so I don't remember talking to them that much."

I had no reason to doubt her for now, but my intuition told me that she was lying.

"There is one more thing," I said, "and it's very important. Do you remember if John was thrown in the river by anyone?"

"Oh, yes!" Moira cried, "how could I forget that?"

"Go on," I said, trying to get as much detail as I could from her.

"Well, I was at home one day, and because I only lived round the corner from John back then, I saw him run past my house, soaking wet. I then went round to his house, with my mother, and we both saw him. He was absolutely drenched.

"What happened?" I asked him.

'They...they made me go into the river', John said to me.

They threw him in, and that made me angry."

This gave Moira a strong motive. I did not want to say anything yet, so I decided to release her.

"Is there anything else you would like to add, because this is the time to do it," I asked her, desperate for more information.

"Well..." said Moira.

I was excited now. We needed as much evidence as we could find.

"There is one thing," said Moira.

"Please, tell me in as much detail as you can," I said.

"There was this one time when John and I were walking by the river alone. This was a few days after that event, so a couple of days before the first murder. We were not far from the river, when we came across the front of a house. It was an old farm house in the distance. I don't even know if people lived there, because I never saw anyone coming in or out of the house. It was in the distance. Anyway, we came up to the path leading up to the house. The path ran in between the field, and John started to get all nervous. He started shaking and everything.

"What's the matter?" I asked him.

"'We did a really bad thing there,' John said to me. He was looking right at the house, so he must have been referring to that place. To this day, I don't know what he meant by that."

That was the most intriguing thing I had heard all day.

"You must have known," I said to her.

"Known what?" an ignorant Moira said.

"That he was the killer," I replied.

"I just denied it. I didn't think that he would be capable of doing something like that," Moira replied, getting up to leave.

That conversation was very interesting, for a number of reasons. We now had a lead, and I knew that the next place I was to go to was that old farm house Moira had mentioned.

Chapter 5

Putting my suspicions about Moira to one side, I set off for the house on my own. This was unusual, but since the others were too busy investigating yet another gang killing, I was the only one left to take charge of this case, which had turned out to be more interesting than I had originally thought, even though I had sensed I was about to be on an adventure.

I drove through Hartfield, and I passed through the estate where John Doe lived. I looked around, and caught glimpses of the people who were there, living their day-to-day life. Strangely, when I drove past some of them, they stopped whatever they were doing and turned round, staring at me. I felt rather threatened by that at first, but then I realized that they must have thought that I was here because of the murders. They had obviously seen Graham and Miranda taking Moira away yesterday, so they must have been very curious about what was going on. I looked in my mirror to see if they still watched, but they had since turned back to doing whatever they were doing.

I then came to Hartfield forest, on the edge of town. This place was out of the way, but some of it was up a height, so when I drove the car through it, I could see a view of the whole town. It was very spectacular. I thought about all of the romantic evenings the teenagers of the town would have had here, knowing fine well that bodies were dumped nearby. I drove round further, and looked around at the forest. It was quite moist in parts, but that was because there were so many trees. I approached a dead end, a built-in car park. I saw that I was the only person visiting the forest today.

Before I left the building, I searched the internet to find out where I was going, because I knew that Hartfield forest was quite a big place. I knew where I was, having been taken here before when I was a child. I could remember bits and pieces, but never a strange house. I saw an old path, that was barely visible, but it was still there, so I decided to follow that. I knew that John and Moira probably walked down that way, because that was the way that led to the river.

I walked along for a few minutes, looking around. I thought to myself, what an awful place to die! Those young boys were just left here, waiting to be found by a dog walker. It was sad, very sad. I tried to think of other things to distract myself. Then, I approached a modern-looking sign pointing to the river. If what Moira said was right, I must have been getting closer. I looked down at the river, and saw that a new path had been put in. It was full of tarmac, and it was obvious that it had just recently been put in. I continued to walk along the old pathway.

Two minutes later, I came to another path, and looking down it, I saw that it was the house Moira had mentioned. It was indeed in the distance, and from the way Moira had described it, nothing had changed for the last twenty years. Just as I was coming towards the house, I tripped over something in the ground. It was a circular piece of metal that was fixed into the ground, and I could not see it because it was covered up by grass. That was just typical. Now, I was covered in mud! I couldn't go up there looking like that now, so I decided to quickly drive back home, and back to the station, hoping that none of my colleagues could see me. Just this once, I would tell a lie to the boss, and say that there was nobody home. I then thought to interview John again, to see what I could get out of him about the house. After all, he was open to me in the first interview, so I was likely to get some information in this interview.

Fortunately, I was able to go home, get changed as fast as I could, and return to work without any of my colleagues noticing.

"What did they say?" said Mitchell.

"Nobody was in, sir," I said, "but I'm going to go back at some point. For now, I'm going to talk to John Doe again about the house," I replied.

"You do that," replied Mitchell, "I hate to say it, but I'm more wrapped up in these gang killings on the other side of Manchester. It's getting out of hand now. I'm going to leave you in charge of the John Doe case."

"You won't regret it, sir," I said, trying to reassure him. I was confident that I was going to get to the bottom of this case. Although it was the most challenging case I had come across in a while, it was not the most challenging ever, and unless something else had come up to throw me off track, I knew that I would be able to manage.

I walked into the interview room again, facing John Doe for a third time. This time, John looked more agitated than before.

"Hello, John," I said to him.

"Hello," he replied, shaking.

"You've had your medication, haven't you?" I asked him, checking to see he had actually taken it.

"Yes," he replied.

"John, I'm here for one reason today. I want to ask you about a particular house."

"A house?" he said, immediately alert.

"Yes. I want to know something in particular."

I could see that John had no idea what I was talking about. He was not faking it, so I had to explain to him.

"Well, Moira, your cousin, has been into the station, and she has told me that one time, a few days before the first murder, you said to her that you did something bad in this house," I said, showing a photograph of the house to him.

John remained silent.

"What was that bad thing?" I asked him.

"I can't remember," he replied, pushing the photograph away.

"Why are you so reluctant to speak, now?" I asked him, frustrated.

"I have nothing to say to you," he replied, looking at me right in the eye, which was unusual for him.

"It's obvious that you're hiding something!" I said, becoming increasingly impatient.

"No," he said, putting his head down.

"Well, then..." I said, thinking of something else to say, "is there anything else..."

"My mother is wondering where I am!" John cried, interrupting me.

"What?" I said, shocked by what John had just said. Moira told me that John's mother was dead, so this was a big shock to me.

"I said, my mother will be at home, worried."

"John, your mother is dead," I said, confused about where he was coming from.

"Why do you think that? My mother is at home right now. None of you people have told her, have you?"

"She died over twenty years ago, John," I said.

"She talks to me every day. She sits with me when Moira is not around. She is a very old lady now, but she does her best to see me every day," John said, his eyes almost shut with imagination.

I decided to leave things there, and stop the interview. Again, I had found another lead, and I knew that I had to push the house business to one side, and focus on John's mother.

Chapter 6

The first thing I had to do was to make sure that John's mother was definitely dead. Although improbable, it was not impossible that his mother was alive. She could have faked her death for a number of reasons. People had done it before, so it would have been no real surprise for me.

I looked on the internet for records of John Doe's birth. I had deduced from what Moira told me that in 1992, John was seventeen or eighteen, meaning he was born in either 1974 or 1975, so I searched for every birth record for a John Doe born in that time frame. Fortunately, there was only one record, for a John Doe born in March 1975. That made him thirty-seven years of age. I thought he was much older than that, but there we had it. I then found out his mother's name. Her first name was Francesca, but there was no mention of the father. Her maiden name, Dealtry, was on the birth certificate. This meant that Francesca was not married when she gave birth to John.

After that, I looked for a death certificate for a Francesca Dealtry. There was one, but that was in 1999, and Moira told me that she had died before the killings, so I looked for a marriage record with Francesca Dealtry. One result came up; Francesca had married a couple of months after John was born, to an Eric Doe, so John's father was in his life. However, I then discovered that Eric had died six years later, meaning that he had been raised by his mother. After some more searching, I discovered that when John was fifteen, his mother was killed, which was also just after he had been diagnosed with schizophrenia. On her death certificate, it said that she had died in a car accident. I searched for a newspaper article detailing events about her death, and I found out some information. Francesca was the driver, and she was giving two friends a lift. She died in the crash, but the other two survived. According to the records, nothing could have been done to save her. She was definitely dead.

After this revelation, I was glad to establish that John's mother was without a doubt dead. This made things more interesting, although I did not want to say this to the others. I was beginning to get excited, because I knew that this case was becoming more and more challenging by the minute. My next stop was John's house. I looked forward to seeing John's house and his way of life, because it may have given me an insight into his character a little more.

Nobody was around, or so it seemed, as I drove up to his house. Moira had given me a key, so I was allowed to look inside. I knocked on the door, to make sure nobody was in. I should not have done that, because it would have given that person the opportunity to run away. I waited for a few seconds, and then I looked inside the window. There was not a sign of life there. It was possible that John was making things up, not imagining things, to throw me off track. However, I did not imagine John as the criminal mastermind, because he did not have to come in and confess today.

I stood around, before deciding to enter the house. Just as I put the key in the lock, I was stopped by a woman, who stood outside the front gate, and greeted me.

"Hello!" she said, in a very friendly manner.

"Hello," I replied, not knowing what else to say.

"Has John done something?" she asked.

"That's official police business," I replied. "Who are you?"

"My name's Libby. I'm an old friend of John's."

That name rang a bell. John had mentioned Libby in the first interview, but I did not tell her that.

"Are you, now?" I asked her.

"Yes," she replied. "John and I have been friends for years, but I haven't seen much of him recently."

"Really? Why's that?" I said, hoping for a little bit more information.

"I've been busy recently. I've volunteered for Dog's Trust. I love animals!"

"Do you?"

"Yes. Do you know, I've spent half the morning rescuing a hedgehog from a drainpipe? And the other day, this cat got a spelk in its paw. Oh, sorry, I'm waffling on now!"

"It's alright," I said, getting bored. "So, how long have you and John been friends?"

"Oh, you're giving me an interview now, are you?" laughed Libby. I liked this woman, because she was rather cheerful and sociable.

"No," I laughed, "I'm just trying to find out a bit more about John, that's all."

"What's this about?" she asked again.

"I can't say, yet," I said, knowing that sooner or later, this whole case would be released into the press.

"It's something serious, isn't it?" asked Libby, looking quite apprehensive.

"What makes you say that?" I asked.

"John's always been a funny one," she said.

"What do you mean?" I asked her.

"I don't really know. He never seemed to fit in with the others."

"I know that he's a schizophrenic."

"Really? I didn't know that!"

"You didn't?"

"Well, I've never really thought about John like that."

"Libby, do you remember Moira? She lives just around the corner."

"Oh, Moira! Yes, I do. Me and her were really good friends when we went to school."

"Do you still see her now?"

"Now and then," Libby replied with confidence, "I say hello to her, and that's it."

"She hasn't been behaving strangely, has she?" I asked her, secretly hoping for an affirmative answer.

"No. Like I said, I don't see her that much. Moira is somebody who tends to keep herself to herself. Like me, she is unmarried, and she does not really do much, not like she used to, anyway."

"She used to go out a lot?" I asked, feeling as though I was getting somewhere.

"Oh, yes! I used to see her all the time," I said, "even at somebody's one hundredth birthday party. She went out at four o'clock that day, and stayed out until twelve, when the other party finished!"

"Really?" I asked. It seemed to me that Moira had a rather strange behavior. Although she seemed perfectly normal when I talked to her, she seemed to have an unusual past.

"Yes! And she used to flirt with everybody, in school. Shortly after Richard's death, she just forgot about him and moved on to somebody else."

It was then when it struck me. Moira and Richard (the fourth victim) were an item? Then I thought even deeper; John said that he wrote a love note to Richard, which lured him into the woods. Was it Moira who wrote that note?

"I need to ask you one more question," I said, "and you might think this is a little bit stupid."

"Not at all," said Libby, "fire away!"

"Well, do you remember years ago, when Richard Cliffe was killed?"

"Yes, I do. It was a sad time, with the others dying, too."

"Well, Richard received a note, which lured him to his death. Do you remember if Moira wrote that note?"

"Yes. She wrote the note and pushed it through Richard's locker. Nobody was looking."

"How do you know this?" I asked.

"Well, she told me."

"Did she now?" I asked.

"Didn't you know? Moira and Richard were an item!"

"This is news to me!" I cried, "and thank you for your time! Also, I would appreciate it if you didn't tell anybody about this, not yet, anyway."

"You have my word," said Libby, waving goodbye to me.

Libby had proved most helpful, even if she didn't realize it. I could not believe what I had heard. In the interview, John said that he was the one who pushed the note through the locker, but I had a witness who claimed otherwise.

I returned to the station, and made a few phone calls, just to verify that Moira and Richard were had dated just before his murder. I made a few calls to people who were in the same classes as Moira and Richard, and also Richard's parents, who confirmed that Moira and Richard were indeed dating at the time of his death. Now, I suspected Moira more than John, and I strongly believed that Moira had something to do with the murders.

Chapter 7

I did not doubt Libby at all. For whatever reason, she knew she got Moira into trouble. Perhaps she did not want to lie to the police, or she accidentally let slip about the note, but she told the truth about it, because other people had confirmed that Moira and Richard were boyfriend and girlfriend at the time of Richard's death. This was something that I needed to think about. Moira had lied in the first place; I had evidence of that and was now ready to put pressure on her. I arrested her for suspicion of the murders, and it was her turn to be formally interviewed.

I entered the room, and she sat as still as a stone, not even a tremor in her hands. Her eyes were barely moving. Perhaps she was traumatized about the whole thing, but I knew that was probably not true.

"So, Moira," I said as I walked through the door, "I am going to ask you again. Did you write Richard that love note the day he died?"

"No, I didn't," Moira said with a very firm tone of voice.

"Well, you see, I have a witness who said you did."

"Who on Earth told you that?!" she yelled, showing that she was confused.

"I'm not allowed to say. Now I'm going to ask you this again. What was your relationship with Richard Cliffe?"

Moira shrugged. "He was only a classmate," she replied.

I almost laughed, because I had testimony that conveyed otherwise.

"You see," I said, "I know for a fact that you are lying to me about that, because I have eight witnesses who will argue otherwise. They say that you were boyfriend and girlfriend until the day Richard died."

"That's bull!" she cried, still attempting to deny things.

"Well, the more you lie to me, the less I trust you," I said, "and to be honest, I have little faith in you now, if any, so you'd better tell the truth, and tell it right now!"

Moira sat there, silent. Her shoulders were right up, and she dropped them, and gave a big sigh.

"OK, I'll tell you the truth this time," she said.

I thought in my head, "finally!"

"Well, Richard and I were dating each other until the day he died. Are you happy now?"

"Did you write the note?"

"I honestly can't remember that! I don't remember little things like that," she said, becoming desperate for me to trust her.

"Well, it is a big thing, actually. Probably the biggest thing in the whole case at the moment, because whoever wrote that note lured Richard Cliffe to his death, so I'm inferring that whoever wrote that note is the Hartfield Hacker."

"I might have wrote it, but I really cannot remember something from twenty years ago!"

"Alright," I said, "but if somebody has said you've written it, and they said they saw you write it, then you probably did write it."

"I understand that. Maybe someone else saw me write the note, and used it to follow Richard to the woods."

"Ah!" I said.

"What?" said Moira, puzzled.

"I did not mention what was in the note!" I cried excitedly, knowing that I had caught her.

Moira knew it as well.

"Please, don't do this," she said, "I promise you, it's nothing to do with the murders."

"But it is," I said, "otherwise, you would tell me."

Moira knew that she had to tell me the whole truth now.

"Well, it's John," she said in a whisper.

"Has he confessed to you?" I asked her.

Moira nodded.

"I didn't want to say anything," she said, "but just before he came to the station the other night, he told me that he was the killer, and how he did it. He told me he was going home. I didn't know he was coming to the police station to confess, though!"

"So, he told you everything about the note?" I asked her.

"Yes! He said he saw me write a note to him, and used that as his opportunity to kill Richard!"

"Right," I said, very interested about the way this story had unfolded.

Now I was back to square one.

"I think I'm done here," I said.

"Can I go now?" she asked me, preparing to get up.

"You do realize that your cousin is still in custody?" I asked her.

"There's nothing I can do for him now, is there?" she asked me.

"No."

"He really is the killer, isn't he?"

I looked at her. Moira was genuinely telling the truth.

"I promise you, I will get to the very bottom of this," I said, "and I know for a fact that there is more to this story than meets the eye. Is there anything else, anything at all, that you want to tell me?"

"I can't think of anything at the moment," she replied with her hands together as though she were in prayer.

"Then you are free to go," I told her.

This was getting more and more puzzling by the minute. So, if what Moira said was true, John was the one who saw her writing the note to Richard, and used that as his opportunity to kill him. I had more to think about in my bed that night, and I knew that for certain.

For now, however, it was time to give John his phone call to someone. About half an hour after Moira went home, John was given his phone call, and I stood right next to him.

He slowly approached the telephone, and I watched him as he dialed the numbers with great care. Staring at the wall, he put the telephone to his ear, and waited not more than two seconds.

"Hello," he said, "oh, yes, I'm fine. Are you alright? I've been so worried about you. No, I don't know when I'll be home. I don't think they'll ever let me out."

He looked at me when he said that.

"I love you, mother," he said, suddenly.

In an instant, I grabbed the phone, and put it to my ear. I did not say anything, but when I put the receiver to my ear, the person on the other end of the line had hung up.

I got very excited now. I had to trace that phone call to make sure that somebody was actually talking to him.

Within ten minutes, another police officer on the team had traced the phone call, and proved that somebody had been on the other end of the line.

"It's Moira," I said, "I just know it's Moira."

"How do you know it's her?" Miranda asked me.

"Because that's the only person he talks to."

I knew that John could have been confused between his mother and Moira, but that also made me believe that Moira could have been pretending to be his mother all along. Either that, or John's mind was just jumbled, unable to distinguish between Moira and his mother. Either way, I inferred that Moira was on the other end of the line. Graham and I telephoned her and asked her for an alibi. She said that she was at home when that happened, about ten minutes before. This meant that nobody could prove where she was at the time, so we were no further forward with the case. Thinking that this direction of the case had come to its end, I decided to turn back to the mysterious house Moira had mentioned before.

Chapter 8

The first thing I knew I had to do was to find out who was living in the house in 1992. I did this by looking up the 1991 census record for the list of occupants. I knew that by finding out who was living in the house at the time, it would bring me one step closer to finding out what the "bad thing" was that John did.

I was shocked by what I learned. Two people, named Joseph and Maria Doe, were both in their sixties at the time. Instinct told me that these people were related to John, possibly grandparents. So, the next step was to search for John's father's parents. They came up with two different names to the ones in the census record.

Then I thought, brother of John's grandfather? This lead me to do some further research. I searched the birth records for John's grandfather, and found out that John's great-grandparents were named Antony and Elizabeth. I then searched for Joseph Doe's parents. Indeed, his parents were also named Antony and

Elizabeth. So, I now had proof that the people who were living in that mysterious house were John's great-aunt and great-uncle. This meant that John would have been able to visit the house on several occasions.

I had so many questions that I wanted to answer, but the most important one was, were these people involved in the murders? It was a possibility, if what John had told me was true. Moira did not know about the owners of the house because she was not related to them; she was related to John because her mother and his mother were sisters.

I did some more research on the internet, and I found out that both Joseph and Maria were now dead, and they had been since 1998. That was another lead gone, I thought. I wanted to know more about these people. I wanted to know more about their personality. Now, the only living person who knew them was John, as far as I knew. I was thinking about talking to him again to find out more about them, but I had something else to do first. I wanted to gather some piece of evidence against these people, something that John could not lie about. If I started to ask him questions, I knew that John might lie about them. At first, I suspected Moira of been the murderer, but now, I could not help but feel that Joseph and Maria Doe were the real killers, framing John to set him up and convincing him that his mother was really alive. Perhaps I was going off track a little, but perhaps not.

Then, I had a thought. If these people died over ten years ago, somebody might have moved in there by now. Is there a chance that John kept going to that house after their deaths. There was only one way to find out.

Within twenty minutes, I found myself back at the house again. This time, I was extra careful not to trip over that hidden lump of metal in the ground. I slowly walked up to the house, quite apprehensive about who I was about to see. What was I going to say to them? How was I going to explain this? I saw that a car was parked outside the house, so somebody definitely lived here, and somebody was inside there right now. I knocked on the door, and a friendly looking woman answered.

"Hello," she said, looking slightly confused about what was going on.

"Hello," I replied, "I am detective Tammy Williams. Don't worry!"

"What's this about, then?" the woman said.

"Well, I know you might be a little bit taken back by this, but I am making an inquiry into the previous owners of this house."

The woman shrugged her shoulders. "I never met them," she said.

"Well, I don't know how to break this to you," I said to her, "but there is a chance that the previous owners of this house were serial killers!"

"What?!" the woman cried, "did you hear that, Dave?"

"What was that, Sherry?" a man asked in the background.

"This is, well, weird!" she cried.

"I know, but there is one thing I need to ask you, and it's quite important."

"Come in if you want," the woman said.

"Thank you," I replied, allowing myself in.

"So, what was it you wanted to ask me?"

"Well, I might need both of you for this," I said, feeling rather tense with the fact that the house I sat in might have once belonged to psychotic murderers.

"Come here a minute, Dave," said Sherry.

"Well, I wanted to know, has there been any strange people coming to this house?"

It did not take Sherry long to reply.

"Well, it was a few years ago now..." she started.

"Go on," I said.

"But I remember it quite clearly because it was that odd!"

"OK."

"Well, this one time, I was in the kitchen, and I got a knock on the door. I answered, and there was this man there. He looked rather shell-shocked when he saw me. It was like he did not expect me to answer. I asked him who he was, and he turned his head and looked at something in the garden. I don't know what. He then nodded his head slightly. It was like there was somebody else there with him, hiding away."

"Right," I said, becoming very intrigued, "can you describe this man for me?"

"Well, not really," Sherry said, "he was just a plain man, really. There was nothing distinctive about him at all. He had a sort of black and gray hair, about average height. That's all I can give you. I'm sorry."

I fully understood what Sherry meant. When I looked at John, I could barely remember his face when I left him, because his face was so easy to forget.

"I need to ask you one more thing," I said.

"Go on then," said Dave.

"In what year did you move to this house?"

"It was 1998," Dave replied.

"Can you give me a month?"

"It was in October."

I was relieved to hear that. Maria Doe had died in September 1998, so it was impossible that somebody could have moved in and moved out within a few weeks.

Before I left the house, Sherry told me something else.

"I almost forgot!" she cried.

"What?" I asked her.

"Well, this one time, I saw and old woman running around our front garden, quite sneakily."

"Really?" I asked, even more intrigued now.

"Yes! I only saw the back of her, but she had grey hair, and wore a yellow cardigan."

"Was she now?"

"I could not believe my eyes!"

"Was this before or after the other event?"

"Well, I think it was before, but I cannot be completely certain."

I smiled. "Thank you, Sherry. You have helped me out a great deal!"

"Really?" said Sherry, "oh, and you'll tell me if these people do turn out to be the killers, won't you?"

"You'll probably see it on the news," I said, leaving.

I was very pleased with the results. I now had much more to work on and to think about.

Chapter 9

I went to work the following morning. So far this week, I was actually enjoying my work. I knew I was getting closer to solving the murders as each day went by. In addition, I had never come across something as challenging as this since before I had joined the team. Originally, I thought that I was going to enjoy my job here at the police force, but it was not the same when there were two rival gangs in the city, and we were the ones trying to take them down. I was fortunate to get away from all that, for a while, anyway.

I was about to start work when a fairly old woman stormed into the station and to my work desk. Although initially, I thought I had never seen her before, I did sort of remember her, perhaps when I was driving through the estate.

"I saw you at the estate!" the woman cried.

"Who are you?" I asked, curious about what this woman had to say.

"My name is Helen Potters, and I live right across the street from John Doe."

"OK," I said, "and why have you come here?" I asked, getting right into it.

"I know that you're investigating John Doe for some reason."

"I am," I replied, "but for now, I can't tell you why."

"I understand that. I don't care about that," she said, in a pushy manner.

"What do you want to say, then? Have you got some information on John Doe that we might not have?" I asked, becoming very impatient with her.

"Yes, I do!" she cried, "and it might help to solve your case!"

"Why don't you sit down and tell me the story, then?" I asked her, not knowing if I had heard what she was about to say before, or whether it was something completely new that would make a great deal of help in the case.

"Well, I was out in the front garden, planting some flowers I bought, and I was talking to Libby. I know that John always goes on and on about his dead mother. Well, I know she's dead! I've seen her dead myself! Anyway, when Libby left, I was the only one in the street, so nobody else saw this. After a minute or two, this car pulled around the corner. I didn't see who was driving it at first. I looked again, and I saw John get out of the passenger seat. I thought nothing of it because someone could have been giving him a lift.

Suddenly, though, this old woman just got out of the car! John then linked arms with her and helped her inside! He then shut the door!"

"Right," I said, "that's very interesting."

"Well, does that help?" the woman said, quite proud with herself.

"It helps a great deal," I said, "but I need to ask you a few more questions about this."

"Go on, then."

"When did this happen?"

"Oh, it was about two weeks ago, now."

"Right," I said, very fascinated by what she had just said, "and can you describe this woman to me?"

"Well, I only saw the back of her, but she had grey hair, and a yellow cardigan."

"A yellow cardigan?" I said, feeling as though it were a eureka moment.

"Yes," Helen simply replied.

"Last question," I said, "can you describe the car for me?"

"Well, I didn't get the license plate, or even the make of the car! I know it was dark red, and that's pretty much it."

"Thank you for your time," I said, letting her out.

I now had more notes to go over, as usual. Do I trust this woman? I knew that she could not be making the whole thing up because two people now have said that there was an old woman with a yellow cardigan around with John. This was amazing. I now knew that somebody had been dressing up as an elderly lady, and it wasn't John! But the question was, why? Why would somebody want to do this? I knew that this person was likely to be the murderer, or had a strong role in the killings.

However, my trail of thought was disrupted, as DI Mitchell told me that I was needed for another case, because the gang situation in Manchester was getting out of control. I just wanted this gang thing wrapped up forever, but it seemed to continue non-stop. I also wanted to get on with the case. I knew it was only going to be for a day. It was a shame, because I now had to focus my thoughts on the gang killings, and not the Hartfield Hacker case.

When the day ended, I received a phone call from someone who I never wanted to see or speak to again: my ex-fiancée, Danny. I hadn't spoken to him for three months, and was glad that he was out of my life. I had once thought that I was going to have a wonderful life with him and that he was the one. He betrayed me. Grudgingly, I picked up the phone.

"What is it?" I asked him, eagerly waiting for a reply down the other end of the line.

"It's Danny," he said.

"I know it's you," I said, with a threatening voice.

"I just called to see how you are doing," he said.

"I thought I was behind you forever!"

"Tammy, the last time I saw you was when you solved the Alesha Christen case, and I told you there and then. You just went, without really discussing it."

"What is there to discuss?" I asked, convinced that I was never going to get back with him. "You were hiding the fact that I was not the one you wished to marry."

"Well, you are!"

"Well, why wait for three months until you call out of the blue, eh?"

"I couldn't find the courage to talk to you," he said, his tone of voice changing to be more sad and persuasive. I imagined the puppy dog look he would pull if we were talking face to face.

"And why do you think that is?" I said, before almost putting the phone down.

"Wait!" he cried.

"What?" I barked at him.

"The reason I broke up with you is because we were spending too much time apart. Why don't we give it one last shot?"

"Even if we did, I would consider my work a top priority in my life. My work is very important to me."

Danny did not reply, even though I could still hear him there as he was breathing down the phone.

"Goodbye, Danny," I said, stopping the phone call and switching the phone off.

I came out of the toilets, and saw that I was not allowed to leave work for another five minutes, so I decided to just forget that phone call and talk to my colleagues about things.

"So, how are you getting on with the Hartfield Hacker case, then?" asked Patricia.

"Well, it's very confusing," I said.

"Do you think it was this mysterious man?" asked Graham.

"I'm not entirely sure yet," I replied, "I have reason to believe that there was someone else involved."

"Why do you think that?" said Miranda, trying not to show that she was jealous of me because I was involved in the case and she was not.

"Well, John's mother is dead, but I have witnesses who claim that they saw an old woman with John on several occasions. I think that there is somebody dressing up as John's mother for whatever reason."

"Why would someone want to do that?" asked Patricia.

"It sounds a little fishy to me," said Graham.

Perhaps I was taking my eye off the ball a little, or perhaps not. I went to bed that evening, unable to sleep because of everything on my mind. I thought about what I was going to do the next day to progress even further in the case.

Chapter 10

The only thing I could do at this point was to research the great-aunt and great-uncle of John Doe. Nothing more could be done, because every other lead that I investigated came to a dead end. I just hoped that everything would soon come together and explain all of this madness. One thing was for certain: I was much closer to solving the murders than anyone was a week before. That was what motivated me to work. I had to admit to myself that this was the most challenging case I had ever come across, because it was just so confusing, and there were so many questions that I could not yet answer.

I did not know why, but something just came over me. I began to think that Joseph and Maria Doe had some sort of criminal history, so I decided to check them for any criminal records. Astonishingly, I was right, and I found out that they were both convicted with attempting to kidnap a six-year old child! I was not prepared for that. I was not prepared for anything, really. I just did not know what to expect with these people. I sensed that there was something wrong there, and I was right. I read the case file further, and they both served four years in prison for it, between the years of 1979 and 1983, so John was actually a child himself. I read even further, and found one of the statements from Joseph Doe.

"We only wanted to kidnap the child because we were desperate for money. We are not pedophiles, and we should only be lightly punished for this. We were in a desperate situation, and we were not going to cause any harm to the girl. We were actually going to make her stay with us very comforting."

There was something extremely fishy about all that. If they were desperate for money, how could they afford to pay for that big house? Of course, I knew in my mind what they were planning to do to that girl, and it was fortunate that she was found just in time. Then I thought, was John subject to this abuse as a child? If so, where was his mother?

Throughout my pondering, the same thing was running through my mind: what was the bad thing that John did in that house? Who did he do it with? I was certain that that had something to do with the murder. However, I only had Moira's word on that, so if she turned out to be the killer, that would have probably been made up to mislead me. I then thought about John again. If he was subject to any kind of abuse when he was a young child, it could have disturbed him for the rest of his life. I then thought to myself, what if he is actually the murderer, and nobody else is involved, and all this investigating has been a waste of time? Then, I thought to myself, no, this is not a waste of time. I have some faith in Moira and John and I will to whatever it takes to prove their innocence and get justice for the families of the victims once and for all!

My next step was to interview John, yet again. I found him sitting in the interview room with a cup of coffee in his hands.

"Hello, again," he said to me with a sigh. His tone of voice was still friendly, but I could tell that he was depressed.

"Are you OK, today, John?" I asked him, taking a soft approach to this.

"I'm fine. I just want to know, why do you keep wanting to talk to me? I've confessed to the murders!"

"There are still things that need wrapping up," I replied in a soft tone of voice.

"But I am the Hartfield Hacker! There is nobody else involved! Why don't you just leave it like that?" John said in an argumentative manner.

"I don't believe you," I told him, "and I think that there is someone else involved. I don't know who yet, but I will definitely find out, no matter what!"

"What do you want to ask me today, then?" said John, sighing again.

"Do you remember your aunt and uncle, Joseph and Moira?" I asked him

John shook his head.

"Perhaps you know them as Uncle and Aunt Doe, or something like that?"

"Well, there was an auntie and uncle I used to visit, in that farm house, but that was years ago," he replied.

"OK, and who did you go with?" I said, with my notebook and pen ready.

"My mother used to take me. My father was rarely there. He used to work in distribution."

"Right, and what were these people like?" I asked him.

"I only went every so often, so I didn't really know them," he replied. John looked very uncomfortable when he said that.

"John, is there something you're not telling me?" I said, detecting his lie.

"No," said a very defensive John.

"There is. I know there is," I said. "Come on, John. You can talk to me."

"Well, there was this one time..."

"Go on," I said, eager for some sort of response.

"It doesn't matter. It has nothing to do with the murders," he said.

"I think it does," I said, getting more and more desperate for him to say something useful.

"Well, one time, my auntie took my mother in the garden for a drink and a chat. I asked my uncle if I could have a drink, and because I didn't say please, he grabbed hold of my neck, and forced me into the cupboard."

"That's horrible!" I cried, determined not to let my emotions get the better of me.

"I know. That went on for a few minutes. There were other times when the pair of them hit me."

"Did your mother find out about this?"

"I think she did, because after that, I stopped seeing them."

"Right, and how old were you when they used to abuse you?" I asked him.

"I was only around five or six."

I paused for a moment, and thought of how evil and horrible these people must have been. I knew that they were now dead, but they did not really have justice brought to them. Although they spent four long years in prison, they deserved more than that.

"There is one more thing I need to go over with you, John," I said.

"I think I know what's coming," John said, almost laughing.

"Well, what was that bad thing you did in that house?"

"I'm telling you, I don't remember!"

I decided to leave it as that. Then John spoke again, which surprised me, because he did not really speak until he was spoken to.

"Can I tell you something?" he said.

"What is it?" I asked, hoping and praying that this had something to do with the case.

"Every time I killed one of those boys, I thought of my aunt and uncle. I imagined I was killing them."

"What makes you say that to me?" I asked him.

"I don't know. I just wanted to get it off my chest," he replied.

I did not reply to that. I left the interview room. I sat down. Nobody else was around at the time, because they were off investigating more gang shootings. I started to cry. It was just a little whimper. It was probably because of the stress and the emotions associated with the case. The whole thing was so sad. After five minutes, I gathered my head together and carried on with my work.

Chapter 11

The next day, I went through each of the four case files once more, as I felt as though I had missed or completely overlooked something important. I looked at the case files as if I was restarting the investigation and none of this had happened. Therefore, I was able to look at all of the facts separately. I picked out the main points from each file and read aloud in my head:

"Josh Dowling was seen at a friend's birthday party. After dancing, he apparently went outside for a cigarette, where nobody ever saw him again. There were thirty witnesses who say they have little memory of the night before. His body had been found in the middle of Hartfield forest, and he had been stabbed seven times. There were no witnesses, and no DNA evidence was collected."

I thought to myself, "it's typical that nobody could remember anything, because they were probably all drunk!"

I then read the next case file in my head:

"Steven Burbery went out for a walk in Hartfield forest with his dog. His mother said that he always loved going on walks, so it was not unusual for him to go into the forest. His mother was alerted by Steven's disappearance when the dog arrived home without him. After telephoning the police, Steven's body was soon discovered in the woods. He had been stabbed six times. Again, there were no witnesses and no DNA evidence."

I then went on to the third one:

"Daniel Gibson was seen leaving school at 4:00pm. His body, along with his school bag and PE kit, was found on Warwick Street, Hartfield. However, it was not until around 6:00pm when his body was discovered by a resident of the street. No witnesses came forward, and no DNA evidence was found. He had been stabbed four times."

And finally, I went on to the fourth one:

"Richard Cliffe was seen leaving school at 4:00pm. His body, along with his school bag, was found in Hartfield forest. He had been stabbed seven times. There were no witnesses, and no DNA evidence was found."

The fourth one was very empty. No more information was given to the parents. That was very sad, I thought.

Whilst I was thinking away, my brain locked in detective mode, something suddenly came over me, and I remembered something that somebody had said earlier. Everything came coming towards me. I looked at one of the case files again, and I realized something. Everything now fit, or almost everything. I had to make one more visit to another person's house to make sure I was right, but I thought I was very close to solving the murder!

"Have you got a spare ten minutes?" I asked Graham.

"Well, yeah. Why?" he asked me.

"Because I've had an eureka moment," I said to him. He did not reply. Instead, he looked at me, very confused.

"I'll come with you, if that's what you're asking."

"Yes. I want you to come."

"Alright," he agreed.

I was getting very excited now, and I knew that something good was coming. The person's house I was going to visit was the mother and father of Steven Burbery, the second victim who went out for a walk with his dog and never came back. Pretty much everything was riding on the answer that this woman gave me, because it was the final piece of the puzzle. Everything else fit perfectly. I just needed some more facts to back my explanation for all this up.

We arrived at the house, and a woman in her sixties answered.

"Are you the police?" she asked.

"Hello, and yes, we are," I said, "are you Mrs. Burbery?"

"Yes, I am," she replied, allowing us inside.

"What's this about this time?" she asked, in a kind manner.

I did not know how to break this to her, so I just said what was on my mind.

"I have one question about your son's death," I said, "and your answer is the most crucial thing in this case!"

"Is it really that serious?" Mrs. Burbery asked.

"I'm afraid it is," I replied.

"What's the question, then?" the old woman asked, clearly trying not to let herself get too excited.

"I want to know, do you remember if your son was a keen dog walker?"

"Oh, yes," she replied, "he loved that dog. He went out with her every day."

"Where did he go?"

"He went to a variety of places. Everywhere he went in Hartfield, it was a new route, because he used to tell me himself that he loved to explore."

That was the answer I was looking for.

"Mrs. Burbery," I said, getting very excited, "I would like you to come with us to the police station."

"Why?" she asked, very puzzled by now.

"I will explain everything when I get there, but I can tell you that I have solved your son's murder!"

"What?!" she cried. She then shouted her husband in from the garden. This woman was ecstatic. I would be, too, because she had been waiting for this day for over twenty years.

"Graham," I said, "I need you to get both Moira and Libby over here. Tell them I need them to verify a few things," I said.

"Moira and Libby who?" he asked me.

"Here's my phone," I said, escorting the woman to the car.

This was it now. I now knew without a doubt who the murderer was, and I was ready to denounce them in front of the parents of the victims and a group of other people.

Chapter 12

We arrived back at the police station, awaiting my denouncement. I did not say anything to Graham yet, though I knew he was eager to know. When we entered the police station, we waited. The first to arrive was John Doe. On the way there, Graham had phoned and asked him to be taken into one of the large interview rooms, where I was going to explain everything to all. The next people to arrive were Moira and Libby.

"What is this about?" asked Libby, "I have things to do!"

"All will be revealed," I told her.

Then, two by two, the parents of the three other victims arrived. Finally, Miranda, Patricia and DI Mitchell stood in the background. Now that everyone was here, I was ready to begin.

"We are here today because I wanted to tell you all who the Hartfield Hacker is. You might not have guessed this, but the murderer is in this very room!"

Many of the parents looked around.

"And I wanted to say to the rest of you, that John Doe is not the Hartfield Hacker!"

This instantly created an uproar of gasps and whispers.

"In a minute, you will know who the real serial killer is, but I just want to point out a few things. First, all of us, including myself, made two assumptions that cost us a lot of time, and threw me in the wrong direction. To see what I am talking about, I need to take you all back to when John and Moira were walking together in the woods. They approached a house. John told Moira that he did a very bad thing there. Those were his exact words. I naturally assumed that the place he referred to was the house, but he wasn't talking about the house at all. In fact, I now know that Joseph and Maria Doe were not involved in the murders in any way, nor was the house."

"So, what was John referring to?" Moira said, interrupting me.

"If you listen, you will know," I replied. "Now, when I went to the house for the first time, I tripped over something. It was a metal stump in the ground. It was of circular shape. Now, just before I visited the house, I saw a sign pointing to the river. I noted that this sign was very modern looking. If you think about it, there must have been a sign somewhere before that one, as it clearly was not twenty years of age. I now know that the sign pointing to the river used to be just outside the farm house."

"What have signs got to do with my son's murder?" asked the father of Richard Cliffe.

"I will explain everything," I replied, "and anyway, it's not the sign, but it's what it pointed to. And what did the sign point to?" I asked Moira.

"The river," she replied.

"Exactly!" I cried, "and that was where John did the 'bad thing'. This takes us to my second wrong assumption. This is the important one. Moira, you told me that you saw John running home one day, dripping wet. Is that true?"

"Yes," replied Moira.

"And what exactly did he say?"

"Well, he said, 'they made me go in the river'."

"Which is exactly what they did," I replied.

"Wait a minute!" said the mother of Daniel Gibson, "you're telling me that our sons threw John into the river?"

"No, I am not saying that at all," I replied. "Now, I am going to reveal who the murderer is, before I go any further."

Everybody fixed their eyes on me. No distraction at all could have forced them to move.

"The murderer is...Libby!"

Everyone turned their heads and stared right at her. Libby looked as shocked as everybody else did.

"Me?" she said in a timid voice.

"Don't try to hide it. I know it was you!" I cried.

"I'm sorry, but you're wrong!" she laughed.

"You know I am not wrong," I said, "and I would like you to keep quiet while I explain everything to everyone. You see, the four murder victims played a small part in the river incident. The person who was thrown in the river was actually Libby. And, from what I just said about the signs and the bad thing, who threw her in?"

"John did," said some of the parents.

"Right, and John dived in right after her, because he realized that she was in danger. You see, these young boys, being teenagers, did not see the danger of throwing somebody into a river. I am guessing that it was quite high up, and Libby did not know how to swim. So, because of the continued bickering, the boys decided that they would taunt John into throwing Libby into the river, little realizing that he would actually do it. And instead of helping Libby, they got scared and ran off, leaving John to save her.

"Libby hated the boys for doing this to her, but she hated John even more for actually throwing her in. So, she made a plan to kill the four boys and frame John, thus getting away with the murders, because nobody would suspect her; as those six were the only ones who knew about that incident, four would be dead and John would be discredited, and Libby would not be suspected by anyone. She would then manipulate John into telling the police that he was the killer. She did this by dressing up as his mother and pretending to be her and developed a mother-son relationship, knowing that, in his current mental state, John would fall for it.

"She would then eventually tell him that she was the murderer, so John would think that it was his mother who did it. I am guessing that Libby then informed him that the police were closing in her, so John was desperate to defend her, and confessed. You all know the rest of the story. It took twenty years, but in Libby's eyes, it was worth every minute."

I paused for a moment to let everybody process what I had just said.

"So, it was Libby who was pretending to be John's mother?" asked Moira.

"Yes. This fits in with everything. Like when I went to John's house. I think that Libby was actually in the house at the time, waiting for a phone call. The knock on the door alerted her, so she sneaked out the back and came to talk to me. She was able to observe Moira going out every day, because she lived just round the corner from her, so she would be able to look from one bedroom window and watch her as she left the house. Whenever Moira did so, Libby would dress up as the old woman and go to the house."

"This is extraordinary!" Patricia said.

"There is more," I said. "When I asked Libby if she knew that John was schizophrenic, or had any mental health disorder, she denied it, even though his illness was blatantly obvious. This was to convince me that she was not trying to manipulate John, or show that she was an easy target."

"What about our son's murders?" asked the mother of Daniel Gibson.

"Well, for the first murder, Libby worked in the club at the time of the party. I know this because before I left the building, I checked the records by telephoning the club. Since she was doing a job that night, Libby was easily able to slip a drug into everybody's drinks. This meant that nobody would be able to remember anything that happened the night before, except for minor details. Furthermore, nobody would suspect a thing because they were all drunk anyway. After the dance, Libby killed him, and put his body into the back of her car. She then waited for people to leave, and dumped his body the forest."

"And the second murder?" said Steven's mother.

"The second murder helped me out a great deal," I said, "because of one thing. I now know that every day, Steven took a new route when he walked his dog, because there was a lot of the town to explore. If Steven walked his dog on a different route every day, would the dog be able to remember everything?"

There were a few shakes of heads.

"A dog's brain is not adapted enough to be that clever, so it would not remember its exact way home. So, how did it get home? The answer is that somebody must have taken it home. Obviously, this person was Libby. After killing Steven, she noticed the dog, and since she cares for animals so much, she drove it home, where she left it to find its own way back."

"And the third?" said Daniel's mother.

"The third murder was quite puzzling, but the answer was very simple. There were no witnesses at the time, were there?"

"No," some people said.

"So, why did Libby take the risk and kill him in an open street. The answer is simple: because she knew that nobody was there. She knew that everybody in Warwick Street was out for a 100th birthday party, or somebody's anniversary. This lasted for hours from the afternoon until late at night. Knowing this, Libby was able to kill Daniel without anybody seeing at all."

I then moved on to the fourth murder.

"The fourth murder was very puzzling indeed, but I now know that it was Libby who wrote the note to Richard, because she knew that Moira and Richard were dating, so Richard would naturally assume that it was Moira who wrote the note. That's all there is to that. I'm finished now, so does anybody have any questions?"

Nobody answered.

"I have one!" cried Libby.

"And what is that?" I said to her.

"How can you prove any of this?" she said with a fairly smug look on her face.

"Please, don't let her get away with it!" one of the parents begged.

"I won't," I replied, "and I do in fact, have evidence. I know that the love note that was written to Richard would have your fingerprints on it. If you are innocent, you would have no need to touch the piece of paper, so they would not be there."

Libby looked very vexed by now.

"Alright!" she cried, "I'm the Hartfield Hacker! Are you all happy now?!"

Moira looked at her. Everyone else looked at her. Patricia was the one who arrested her.

A couple of minutes later, everybody prepared to leave.

"Thank you so much!" cried the parents of the victims, "we've waited twenty years for this day!"

"I'm glad you've finally found justice," I said, "and Libby will never get out of prison again. That is guaranteed."

"I never thought it would be a woman," said the father of Daniel Gibson, "I thought about who the killer might be a lot, and I prayed to God for that day. Without you, we would have never found true justice!"

The parents left. However, there were still two people I wanted to speak to. Moira slowly approached us.

"Thank you," she said, almost crying.

"What for?" I asked.

"For having faith in us."

Moira and John then held hands, and walked out of the police station and into the sunlight. I almost cried when I watched them give each other a hug.

"It's over now," said Moira, "it's all over."

And I'm glad it is!

About the Author

Brie Krauss lives in the United States with her family. Though not planning on becoming a writer, she had a few murder mysteries rolling around in her head and decided to write them on day, mostly so she could stop thinking about them. Always a fan of novellas, and quick entertainment, she kept the Closed Case stories short on purpose and hopes you enjoy them.

More from Brie Kraus

Closed Case

Curious Confession
Murder on the Eiffel Tower
Over The Hills

Other Books

Don't Ask
I Hate You Rock Stars